D0339653

CALGARY PUBLIC LIBRARY

NOV    2015

# JIM NASIUM

**STONE ARCH BOOKS**
a capstone imprint

Jim Nasium
is published by Stone Arch Books,
a Capstone Imprint
1710 Roe Crest Drive
North Mankato, Minnesota 56003
www.capstoneyoungreaders.com

Copyright © 2016 Capstone.
All rights reserved. No part of this publication may be reproduced
in whole or in part, or stored in a retrieval system, or transmitted in
any form or by any means, electronic, mechanical, photocopying,
recording, or otherwise, without written permission of the publisher.

Cataloging-in-Publication Data is available on
the Library of Congress website.
ISBN: 978-1-4965-0522-4 (reinforced library bound)
ISBN: 978-1-4965-0527-9 (paperback)
ISBN: 978-1-4965-2331-0 (eBook)

Summary: Jim Nasium is desperate to live up to his name and find
the perfect sport to suit his yet-to-be-discovered skills! This time Jim is
trying his luck on the gridiron. But how can Jim test his football skills
when his schoolyard enemies are all on the starting lineup? When a
late-game injury takes a player off the field, it's up to Jim Nasium,
backup quarterback, to win the championship game!

Printed in the United States of America in Stevens Point, Wisconsin.
052015        008824WZF15

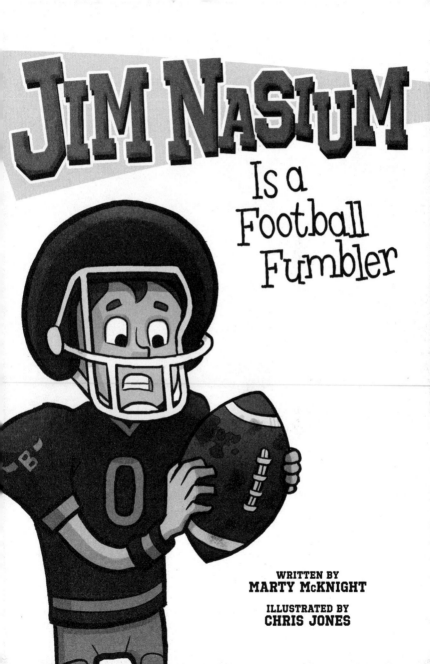

# JIM NASIUM
## Is a Football Fumbler

WRITTEN BY
**MARTY McKNIGHT**

ILLUSTRATED BY
**CHRIS JONES**

# CONTENTS

# CHAPTER ONE

# FRESH START

I sat inside the school locker room with a dozen other boys. I nervously chewed at my fingernails and then stopped. *Do star quarterbacks trim their nails before a big game?* I wondered. Better not chance it.

It was the first day of football, and this was going to be my season.

Coach Pittman entered the room. He placed a large cardboard box on a bench and quickly stepped back. Everyone rushed over to take a look.

I pushed through the crowd and saw that the box was filled with brand-new football jerseys. They were black with shiny gold numbers.

"Take your seats," the coach shouted. "Don't be animals!"

"But we are animals, Coach," said my best friend, Milo. "We're the Bennett Elementary Buffaloes!" Milo placed two fingers near his head like horns. He bent down and charged at me with a loud **SNORT!**

"All right, all right," Coach interrupted. "Save it for the field."

Everyone quickly took their seats.

"When I call your name, step up and grab a jersey." Coach Pittman pulled out a clipboard and a pen. "Bobby Studwell," he said, checking off the first name on his list.

Milo and I leaned in to each other and groaned. *Of course he'd get to go first,* I thought. *He's picked first for EVERYTHING!*

Bobby strutted toward the box. He sifted through the jerseys and then proudly held up his pick. "A perfect ten, as always," he boasted.

Milo and I groaned louder.

"Okay, take your seat, Bobby," said Coach, rolling his eyes. He looked at his clipboard again. "Tommy Strong."

As usual, Tommy followed Bobby, choosing the number nine from the box.

"Milo Cabrera," Coach called next.

"Yes!" exclaimed Milo, jumping up from the bench. He quickly chose jersey number seven from the box.

"Lucky number seven, huh, Milo?" Coach Pittman asked.

"Luck has nothing to do with it, Coach," he replied.

"Then why'd you choose that number?" asked Coach.

"Because," Milo explained. He pointed at Tommy, staring and chomping his teeth. "Everyone knows that seven *ate* nine!"

Everyone laughed.

Coach shook his head and continued calling names until he finally looked up from his clipboard at me. "And last but not least . . ." he began, marking off the final name with his pen, "Jim Nasium."

\*\*\*

You heard him right. The name's Jim Nasium — don't wear it out!

With a name like mine I should be a sports sensation. You know, a real gym class hero!

The problem is . . . I lack some serious game.

You've heard that old saying "born with two left feet." Well, I was born with two left feet AND two left arms! That's a real problem in football — or any sport, for that matter.

And I'd know. At this point, I've tried just about every sport on the planet.

The result?

Well, let's just say I've warmed some very nice benches in my day.

But this year is going to be different.

This year, I won't be a football fumbler. I'll be a gridiron star!

CHAPTER TWO

# A BIG ZERO

Moments later, the team ran out of the locker room and onto the practice field. Our fresh new jerseys shined in the afternoon sun.

"That number suits you perfectly, Nasium." Bobby laughed and pointed at the big golden zero on my chest.

"Haha! Very funny, Bobby," I replied.

"No, he's right, Jim," Milo said. "A zero has nowhere to go but up!"

**BREEEEEP!** Coach Pittman's whistle suddenly blared. "Hustle up, boys!" he shouted. "We've got a lot of work to do."

Everyone huddled around Coach, taking a knee on the cool grass.

"We had a great season last year," said the coach, pacing back and forth in front of us. "And, as I always say, don't fix something that ain't broken. Everyone will keep their same positions this year."

*Great,* I thought. *Another year as first-string benchwarmer.*

"Bobby Studwell will lead the team as quarterback," Coach Pittman continued, "but we're going to need a backup. Do I have any volunteers?"

Bobby's hand quickly shot up. "I'll do it, Coach!" he said.

"Bobby, you can't play backup for yourself," Coach explained.

"Why not, Coach?" asked Bobby. "Who else is gonna fill these shoes?" He stood and started spinning and twisting in front of the team, showing off his fancy football footwork.

A few kids laughed, but I wasn't paying attention. *This is going to be my season,* I thought again.

And before I could think any better, my hand shot into the air.

"Jim Nasium!" Coach exclaimed, writing my name on his clipboard.

"Ha! Are you serious?" spit Bobby. "He stinks!"

"Well, then he'll definitely be able to fill your shoes, Bobby," Milo interrupted, "because *they* stink, too!"

The team erupted in laughter.

**BREEEEEEEP!**

Coach blew his whistle again. "Settle down, everyone!" he shouted.

Then the coach reached into his equipment bag.

Coach pulled out a slick new football and turned to me. "All right, Jim. Let's see what you can do," he said, tossing me the ball.

I quickly stood and put out my arms. **WHUMP!** The football hit me right in the golden zero on my chest and fell to the grass at my feet.

"This should be good," muttered Bobby.

CHAPTER THREE

# FIRST-STRING FUMBLER

After a few instructions from the coach, the team took the practice field. I led the offense to one side of the fifty-yard line, and Bobby led the defense to the other side.

"You're going down, Nasium!" Bobby shouted, grunting and flexing his biceps at me.

"You're right, Bobby," said Milo, standing by my side. "We are going down — down the field!"

"Good one, Milo," I muttered.

**BREEEEEP!** Coach whistled from the sidelines. "What are you doing, Studwell?!" he shouted at Bobby. "Get over here and take a knee!"

"But, Coach," Bobby pleaded, "I wanna sack Nasium!"

"Not a chance," said the coach as Bobby lumbered off the field, hanging his helmet. "I can't have my star QB getting hurt before the first game."

Then Coach Pittman turned his attention toward me.

"Okay, Nasium, let's pretend it's third down with seven yards to go. Your team is up by three points in the fourth quarter. What do you do?"

"Yes, sir!" I exclaimed. I buttoned my helmet's chinstrap and gathered the offense into a huddle.

Seconds later, Milo spoke up. "Ahem!" he grunted, jabbing his elbow into my ribs. "Jim, you gotta call a play . . ."

"Oh, right," I said.

A moment passed.

"May I suggest a passing play?" Milo offered.

"Works for me," I replied.

After another moment, Milo spoke up again. "Did you have a specific passing play in mind, Jim?" he prodded.

"Oh!" I exclaimed. "I thought *you* were going to suggest one!"

Everyone laughed.

"Tell you what," Milo began, "why don't I just snap the ball, and you work some of that Jim Nasium magic?"

I nodded and then extended my hand into the center of the huddle. Ten other players piled their hands on top of mine.

"Buffaloes on three," I prompted. "One, two, three . . ."

"BUFFALOES!!" the offense shouted back. They broke from the huddle and took their places on the fifty-yard line.

Milo crouched over the ball in the center position, and I quickly moved in behind him. "Hut one! Hut two!" I called out, preparing for the snap. "HUT THREE!"

## CRASH! SMASH! CRUNCH!

Helmets and pads collided as the football hit my fingertips. I took a few steps backward and then looked downfield for an open receiver, but I couldn't find one.

"Throw it, Jim!" yelled Milo, trying to hold off the defense.

Suddenly, one of the receivers broke free from his defender. He sprinted across the center of the field, ten yards away. My eyes grew wide as I pulled the football behind my ear, ready to hit my open teammate with a spiral.

Then . . . **WHAM-O!**

A shiny, black-and-gold helmet struck me right in the gut. I felt the football slip from my hand as I fell to the ground. Players piled on top of me, one after another after another after another after another (plus a couple more).

I could hear cheering and shouting.

Finally, Coach Pittman pulled me from the pile.

"What happen?" I asked him.

The coach pointed toward the opposite end zone. A defensive player was strutting around like a chicken, squawking and celebrating his fumble recovery for a touchdown.

Coach patted me on the back. "Good effort, Nasium," he said.

But I knew what he really meant.

"So much for that Jim Nasium magic," I told Milo as I headed toward the sidelines.

"What are you talking about, Jim?" said Milo. "You just made our three-point lead *disappear*!" He snapped his fingers and smiled.

I couldn't help but smile back.

Just then, Bobby passed me on his way onto the field. "Watch and learn, Nasium," he said, strapping on his helmet and heading toward the line of scrimmage.

He tucked in behind Milo and smoothly called out, "Wide right nine Charlie B on four!"

I didn't understand a word of it.

"HUT! HUT! HUT! HUT!" Bobby shouted, and the play began.

I watched as the wide receivers quickly broke free from their defenders. Bobby didn't hesitate. He pulled his arm back and then released a perfect spiral. The football rocketed through the air before coming back to Earth and striking Tommy Strong right on his jersey number.

Coach Pittman raised his arms into the air. "Touchdown!" he cheered.

Bobby pumped his fist in celebration. Then he turned, pointed toward me on the sideline, and winked.

I unbuttoned my chinstrap and removed my helmet.

Then I took a seat on the cold, metal bench behind me. *This bench could use a good warming anyway,* I thought.

# CHAPTER FOUR

# ARE YOU KITTEN ME?

That night after practice, I was starving. Dinner wasn't ready when I got home, so I headed to my room and plopped down on the bed.

## WHUMP!

My crazy cat, Vinnie, leaped onto my stomach, looking for some attention.

"Ow!" I cried out. "Take it easy, boy!" Even though I'd only played one down of football, every muscle ached.

I stroked Vinnie's black fur and told him about that afternoon's practice. His sharp, pointy claws poked through my T-shirt and into my chest. I noticed my own chewed-up fingernails.

"Maybe if I had claws like you, I wouldn't be such a butterfingers," I told him. "Or maybe . . ."

I tossed Vinnie onto my pillow and then leaped out of bed. I dug through piles of homework, comic books, and action figures until I found my old foam football.

"Maybe," I repeated, gripping the ball in my hand, "I just need to be faster. You know, like a cat!"

I cradled the football in my arm like a professional running back. I raced around the room, leaping onto the bed and then off again. Vinnie's eyes darted back and forth with me.

A moment later, my mom opened the bedroom door. "Dinner's ready, Jim," she said, peeking inside.

"Mom, go long!" I shouted.

Just like in practice, I pulled the football up behind my ear. Then I flung my arm forward, firing a foam missile toward Mom.

"MEOW!"

Suddenly, Vinnie leaped off the bed and swatted the football out of the air with his paws! Mom and I watched as the cat landed and quickly tore the foam ball to pieces with his razor-sharp claws.

"Good effort, Jim," Mom said and then closed the bedroom door behind her.

I had lost my appetite.

CHAPTER FIVE

# SACK LUNCH

## MUNCH! MUNCH! MUNCH!

The next day, I sat with Milo inside the school cafeteria, scarfing down my bag lunch. My mom had packed me a leftover meatloaf sandwich from last night's dinner.

"What's the hurry, Jim?" asked Milo.

I explained how Vinnie had ruined my appetite the night before.

"Sounds like a real *cat*-astrophe," Milo joked.

"I'm serious, Milo," I told him. "If an overweight cat can intercept my passes, how will I ever quarterback this team?"

"You won't," said a voice from behind.

Milo's eyes went wide, and he pointed over my shoulder. I turned and spotted Bobby Studwell and Tommy Strong standing behind me, holding trays of steamy chicken nuggets, mashed potatoes, and gravy.

"What do you mean, Bobby?" asked Milo. "Coach Pittman told Jim that he could be our backup quarterback."

Bobby and Tommy laughed.

"That's only because Coach knows that his star QB never gets injured," Bobby explained. He grabbed a chicken nugget from his tray. "This nugget has a better chance of playing quarterback on Friday." Bobby tossed the chicken nugget into his mouth, chomping on the rubbery meat until it was gone.

"Besides," Bobby added, "can you imagine Nasium leading our team against the Gators? He'd be —"

"SACK LUNCH!" Tommy interrupted, snatching my empty lunch bag from the cafeteria table.

"Haha! Good one, Tommy!" Bobby exclaimed.

"Hey, gimme that back," I shouted.

"Here," said Tommy, crumpling the empty bag and tossing it in my direction. "Catch!"

I watched the greasy brown bag float toward me. My hand shot up like a cat's paw, and I successfully snagged the bag from the air.

Bobby and Tommy looked on, surprised.

"Nice catch, Jim!" Milo exclaimed. Then he gave me a congratulatory pat on the back. **THWACK!** The crumpled bag slipped from my fingers and skittered across the cafeteria floor.

"FUMBLE!" shouted Tommy. He dived onto the floor, grabbed the brown bag, and then hoisted it into the air like a trophy.

The cafeteria erupted in laughter.

Bobby placed his hands on his hips, bent down next to me, and gave me his best Coach Pittman impression.

"Save it for the field, Nasium," he said, snickering.

I hung my head, staring down at the half-eaten meatloaf sandwich.

I had lost my appetite . . . again.

# CHAPTER SIX

# GATOR BAIT

Most days, the players met Coach Pittman on the practice field after school. But today, we gathered inside the locker room for a team meeting.

"Take a seat, gentlemen," Coach said as we shuffled inside. He finished writing a pattern of Xs and Os on a chalkboard. Then he turned toward us and shouted, "Are you ready?"

"Yes, sir!" Bobby exclaimed, hooting and clapping with excitement. A few others nodded and agreed.

"I can't hear you!" the coach yelled, cupping his hand to his ear. "ARE. YOU. READDDDDY?!"

"YES, SIR!" we all replied.

"Good," said Coach. "Because tomorrow we're going to send those Gators packing."

"See you later, Alligators!" Milo joked.

I giggled a bit and so did the rest of the team.

"Laugh now, Cabrera," Coach Pittman began, "because tomorrow you have some serious competition."

The coach removed three pictures from a folder and hung them on the chalkboard with buffalo-shaped magnets. "Meet three of our opponent's defensive linemen, Hugh, Lou, and Stew — better known as the Triple Threat!" he said, pointing to the photos.

"Those players are Gators? They look like high schoolers," Milo exclaimed. "That middle kid has a mustache!" He stroked his bare upper lip, looking nervous.

"Last season, they broke the record for the number of sacks in a single season," Coach continued, "and they only played one game."

"Why's that, Coach?" I asked.

Coach adjusted his whistle and gulped. "They were suspended for tackling their own coach," he said.

Coach Pittman hung up a picture of the Gators' coach. He had a black eye, two missing teeth, and a broken arm in a sling.

We all groaned.

"Don't worry, gentlemen," began the coach. "We have our own secret weapon."

"Aw shucks, Coach. You're embarrassing me," said Bobby, stroking his thick blond hair.

"Not you, Studwell," said the coach. He pulled a piece of chalk from his pocket and turned toward the board. "Good old-fashioned teamwork."

With a screech of the chalk, Coach Pittman feverishly began drawing arrows on the board. He connected the Xs and Os and shouted out rapid-fire plays like an auctioneer.

I listened closely and stared up at the board. Coach had drawn one letter O near the edge of the chalkboard, away from all the other Os and Xs.

It looked lonely and out of place.

I stared at the lonely O for a few moments. Then suddenly, the letter started looking like something awfully familiar.

*A zero,* I thought. *How perfect.*

CHAPTER SEVEN

# THE PURR-FECT PLAN

"What are we doing here?" I asked Milo.

We stood in my backyard after practice. Milo held a big red ball of yarn in one hand and a small, crinkly plastic bag in the other.

"I thought you could use some extra practice before the big game tomorrow," Milo replied.

"But why?" I wondered. "Last I checked the offense only needs eleven players. And eleven minus a zero is still eleven."

"Well yeah, that's true," said Milo, scratching his chin and squinting his eye. "But eleven TIMES a zero is ZERO!"

"What's your point?" I asked.

"The point is . . . I'm smart." He smiled.

I laughed. Milo always knew how to make me feel better.

"Okay, whatever," I said. "But what's with that stuff?" I pointed at the strange items in his hands.

Milo held up the red yarn. "Oh, this is just a regular old ball of yarn," he explained. Then he held up the crinkly plastic bag. "And this is sweet, delicious . . . catnip."

Milo opened the small plastic bag and sprinkled the green flakes of catnip onto the yarn ball. Then he placed two fingers into his mouth and let out an ear-piercing whistle.

**WHEEEEEEEEE!**

"Vinnie! Here, Vinnie!" Milo called.

A split second later, I heard the back door of the house creak open. Then my cat Vinnie appeared through the crack.

His eyes grew wide. His pupils grew black. He let out a long, hungry "Meowwww!"

Then **_WHOOSH!_** He leaped onto the lawn and sprinted straight toward Milo and the catnip-covered yarn.

"Jim, catch!" Milo shouted. He threw the red ball of yarn in my direction, and I instinctively reached up and caught it. "Now run!"

I looked down at the ball of yarn in my hands. Then I looked back up at Vinnie. He had a new target: ME!

"AH!" I screamed, and then I took off running.

I leaped over a lawn chair, spun through my mom's rose garden (OW! OW!), and ran in circles. Vinnie nipped at my heels the whole way.

"Stop him, Milo! Stop him!" I screamed.

Milo laughed and then let out another whistle. **WHEEEE!** "It's third down with seven yards to go," he said. "Your team is up by three points in the fourth quarter. What do you do?"

"HUH?!" I shouted.

"What do you do, Nasium?!" Milo repeated.

I didn't hesitate. I pulled my arm back and released a perfect spiral. The red yarn rocketed through the air and struck Milo right in the chest. A puff of green catnip exploded onto his flannel shirt.

Milo caught the yarn and then raised his arms into the air. "Touchdown!" he exclaimed.

"Meow!" cried Vinnie.

The cat leaped at Milo like a feline linebacker (a feline-backer?) and tackled him onto the grass. Vinnie ripped and chewed at Milo's catnip-covered shirt.

"Ow! Help!" he shouted, trying to pull off the cat.

I laughed. "Real smart, Milo," I said.

## CHAPTER EIGHT

# GAME DAY

The next day, the team met in the locker room again. Everyone started suiting up for the big game.

Coach Pittman noticed the scratches on my arms and on Milo's chest.

"What happened to you two?" he asked.

"A rosebush, sir," I said.

"A cat, sir," Milo followed.

Coach rolled his eyes. "Just hurry up and get those pads on," he said. "The game is about to start!"

Moments later, the Bennett Elementary Buffaloes stampeded onto the field. Hundreds of fans (okay, maybe half a dozen moms, including my own) cheered us on.

As we took our places on the sidelines, the ground began to shake.

## RUMMMMBLE!

I looked over my shoulder and saw the Gators charging toward their sideline, led by Hugh, Lou, and Stew — the Triple Threat!

"Which one's which?" Milo asked.

"Does it matter?" I said. "They're all twice your size."

"And now they ALL have mustaches!" he added.

**BREEEEEP!** Coach Pittman blew his whistle. "Huddle up, gentleman." We all gathered around. "Remember what I told you," he began, "no one here can win this game alone —"

"Ahem!" Bobby interrupted. "No one, Coach?"

"Not even you, Studwell," the coach replied. "This game takes good old-fashioned teamwork, and we've got that. Now let's get out there and say 'See you later' to those Alligators!"

Milo smiled.

Then the coach placed his hand into the center of the huddle. We piled our hands on top.

"Buffaloes on three," the coach shouted. "One, two, three . . ."

"BUFFALOES!!"

The team sprinted onto the field, and we all took our positions. Mine, of course, was the seated position . . . on the bench.

CHAPTER NINE

# DOWN AND OUT

Throughout the first three quarters of the game, the score remained tied at zero. Neither team could reach the end zone. The Triple Threat shut down Bobby, and our defense kept the Gators from biting. It was gridiron gridlock.

Then, on the first play of the fourth quarter, Bobby tucked in behind Milo at the line of scrimmage.

He called out, "Wide right nine Charlie B on four!"

I'd heard that play before, and this time I knew just what to expect.

"HUT! HUT! HUT! HUT!" Bobby shouted.

Milo snapped him the ball, and Bobby quickly drop back three steps. From the sidelines, I could hear Hugh, Lou, and Stew huffing and grunting as they pushed their way through our defense.

Bobby scrambled.

He zigged and zagged, narrowly escaping the hulking arms of the Triple Threat!

Then he looked downfield. I followed his eyes and spotted Tommy Strong sprinting down the sidelines. Bobby saw him, too. He cocked his arm back and fired a bullet forty yards through the air.

Without breaking stride, Tommy Strong stretched his arms out in front of him. The football landed perfectly on his awaiting fingertips. Two steps later he was in the end zone!

The referee raised his arms above his head, signaling a touchdown. Bobby celebrated with his now-patented fist pump. The rest of the team ran back to the sidelines, hooting and hollering.

"Gather 'round, boys," said Coach Pittman as the team huddled up. "A couple more plays like that and pizza's on me tonight!"

Everyone cheered.

Then the coach pulled out his clipboard and started drawing up a play. I moved in closer, peeking over his shoulder for a better look.

"Back up," said Coach.

"Yes, sir? What do you need? I'm ready to go in, sir," I said, excited to play some backup quarterback.

"No, Jim, I meant move back a bit. I need a little space, son," the coach explained.

"Oh, right," I said, stepping aside.

"Yeah, Jim, take a seat," added Bobby. "We got this game in the bag. Isn't that right, Tommy?"

"Like a meatloaf sandwich," Tommy joked.

Bobby and Tommy snickered.

Then, team headed back onto the field to kick the extra point.

"Don't worry, Jim," said Milo, strapping his helmet back on. "At least you don't have to face the Triple Threat!"

\*\*\*

As the game neared the end of the fourth quarter, I thought about what Milo had said. He was right. On the sidelines, I didn't have to worry about the Triple Threat or fumbling or being intercepted by a cat. Our team had the ball. We were up by three points, 13–10, and soon the game would be over. I could just sit back on this safe, cool bench and relax . . .

**BREEEEEEEEP!**

Just then, the referee sounded his whistle. I looked up and saw Hugh, Lou, and Stew in a hog pile on our seven-yard line. When they finally peeled themselves off of each other, I spotted Bobby lying on the ground.

Bobby slowly stood, clutching his knee. He hobbled to the sideline with the help of Tommy and Milo. He took a seat on the bench next to me.

Bobby looked bad. His knee was swollen, blood dripped from his nose, and the golden number one on his jersey was half peeled off.

A moment later, I felt a hand on my shoulder pad and looked up.

"All right, Jim," said Coach Pittman. He shoved a dirty football into my gut. "Let's see what you can do."

# CHAPTER TEN

# ZERO TO HERO

Before I could think better, I trotted onto the field, holding my helmeted head high. *Maybe this is my season,* I thought, feeling surprisingly confident. *Maybe I'll finally earn some respect.*

"Yoo-hoo!" came a sudden call from the bleachers.

I looked up and spotted my mom in the stands. She was holding up a large, colorful sign.

It read, "JIM NASIUM IS A ZERO!" Only she'd crossed out the Z and added an H above it, so instead the word read "HERO!"

"Mommy loves you, sweetheart!" she exclaimed.

Hugh, Lou, and Stew laughed until their giant-sized bellies jiggled.

"Well, that was embarrassing," said Milo as I entered the huddle.

"Thanks for pointing that out, Milo," I replied. "I hadn't noticed."

Milo gave a joking smile. Then he turned and pointed up at the scoreboard. "Hey, Jim, check it out!" he said.

I looked up at the scoreboard. It was third down with seven yards to go and our team was up three points in the fourth quarter.

"What do you do?" he said, giving me a knowing wink.

"Third time's charm, right, Milo?" I smiled.

I called a play, and we broke from the huddle. The offense spread out across the seven-yard line, and I took my place behind Milo.

"HUT! HUT! HUT!" I shouted, and Milo snapped the football.

## CRASH! SMASH! CRUNCH!

The Triple Threat quickly broke through our offensive line. Their eyes grew wide. Their pupils grew black. They each let out a hungry growl.

I scrambled for my life. I leaped over Hugh, spun past Lou, and ran in circles around Stew.

Then, seven yards away in the end zone, I spotted a bright, gold number seven shining in the afternoon sun. I pulled the football up behind my ear, ready to pass to Milo. Then . . . **FWIP!**

The football suddenly slipped from my buttery fingers. It skittered across the field and into the end zone like a greasy paper bag.

"FUMBLE!!" I heard someone cry out.

I dived toward the bouncing ball in what felt like a slow-motion replay. Twenty-one other players joined me in the pile.

A few moments later, I could hear cheering and shouting. I could feel the weight lifting from the pile. Then a hand pulled me to my feet.

It was Milo.

"What happen?" I asked him.

Milo pointed at the referee nearby. The arms of his black-and-white striped shirt were raised above his head.

Then I looked down at my own arms. Cradled between them was a football. The game-winning football.

"You did it!" Milo exclaimed.

"We did it, Milo," I told him, although I knew it was kind of a cheesy thing to say.

The rest of the team stampeded onto the field. They cheered, slapping me on the helmet and shoulder pads.

Bobby hobbled up behind them. As he approached, the number one on his jersey peeled completely off. It fell to the ground at his feet. Only a big golden zero remained on Bobby's chest.

Milo reached down and picked up the number one. He stuck it to the right of the zero on my jersey. "Number one!" Milo exclaimed. "Like I said, Jim, when you're a zero, there's nowhere to go but up."

I smiled. But then I tore the number one from my jersey. I ripped off the zero, too. "Nobody here's a zero or a one or a ten," I said. "We're all Buffaloes!"

Everyone cheered.

Then Bobby peeled the remaining zero from his jersey. Tommy followed with his nine. Then Milo and the rest of the team started peeling off there own numbers.

"ACK!" screamed the coach. "There's three minutes left in this game, and those are brand new jerseys! What are you doing?"

"It's called good old-fashioned teamwork, Coach," Milo explained.

The coach dropped his clipboard, shook his head, and headed back to the sidelines.

Three minutes later, we won the game, beating the Gators 20–10. But that number didn't matter either.

Even without the zero on my chest, I knew I was still a football fumbler. But for at least one day, one play, I was also a gridiron star!

# AUTHOR

Marty McKnight is a freelance writer from St. Paul, Minnesota. He has written many chapter books for young readers.

# ILLUSTRATOR

Chris Jones is a children's illustrator based in Canada. He has worked as both a graphic designer and an illustrator. His illustrations have appeared in several magazines and educational publications, and he also has numerous graphic novels and children's books to his credit. Chris is inspired by good music, books, long walks, and generous amounts of coffee.

# FOOTBALL JOKES!

**Q: What football team travels with the most luggage?**

A: The Packers!

**Q: What football team spends the most money on their credit cards?**

A: The Chargers!

**Q: Why is a football stadium always so cool?**

A: Because it's full of fans!

**Q: What dessert should offensive football players never eat?**

A: Turnovers.

**Q: What do you do when you see an elephant with a football?**

A: Get out of his way!

**Q: What did the football coach say to the broken candy machine?**

A: Give me my quarterback!

**Q: Why did the football player wear his pads to the library?**

A: The teacher told him to hit the books!

JIM NASIUM IS A Football Fumbler

BY MARTY McKNIGHT & CHRIS JONES

JIM NASIUM IS A Basket Case

BY MARTY McKNIGHT & CHRIS JONES

JIM NASIUM IS A Soccer Goofball

BY MARTY McKNIGHT & CHRIS JONES

JIM NASIUM IS A Hockey Hazard

BY MARTY McKNIGHT & CHRIS JONES